My Little Album of Dublin

M'ALBAM BEAG DE BHAILE ÁTHA CLIATH

AN ENGLISH/IRISH WORDBOOK

LEABHAR FOCAL BÉARLA/GAEILGE

Juliette Saumande & Tarsila Krüse

THE O'BRIEN PRESS
DUBLIN

ON O'CONNELL STREET

Ar Sráid Uí Chonaill

Signs
Comharthaí

Busker
Buscálaí

Door
Doras

Bus stop
Stad Bus

Post box
Bosca poist

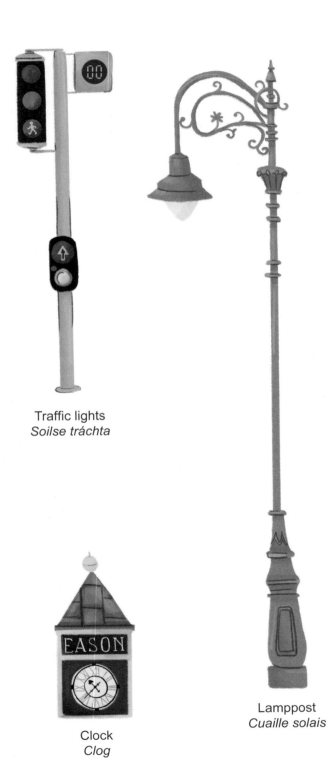

Traffic lights
Soilse tráchta

Clock
Clog

Lamppost
Cuaille solais

Shop
Siopa

Pigeon
Colúr

Dublin bike
Rothar Bhaile Átha Cliath

On the DART
Ar an DART

LEAP Card
Cárta LEAP

Bin
Bosca bruscair

Billboard
Clár fógraí

Display
Scáileán

Turnstile
Geata casta

Change
Sóinseáil

Luggage
Bagáiste

Passengers
Paisinéirí

Schoolbag
Mála scoile

Copy and pencil
*Cóipleabhar agus
peann luaidhe*

Books
Leabhair

Toilets
Leithris

Skipping rope
Téad scipeála

Computer
Ríomhaire

Lunch box and snack
*Bosca lóin agus
sneaic*

9

At the
Zoo
Ag
an
Zú

Orang-utan
Óran-útan

Flamingo
Lasairéan

Insect hotel
Ostán feithidí

Stick insect
Cipíneach

Snow leopard
Liopard sneachta

Deer
Fia

Zookeeper
Coimeádaí zú

Humboldt penguin
Piongain Pheiriúch

Sloth
Spadán

Peacock
Péacóg

Kiosk
Both

Map
Mapa

African painted dog
Gadhar seilge Afracach

Sealion
Mór-rón

Chameleon
Caimileon

At the Museum

Ag an Músaem

Butterflies at the Natural
History Museum
*Féileacáin ag Músaem
Stair an Dúlra*

Jewellery
Seoda

Eileen Gray chair
Cathaoir Eileen Gray

High cross from The National
Museum – Decorative Arts & Hist...
*Cros ard ón Ard-Mhúsaem – Na
hEalaíona Maisiúla & Stair*

The Book of Kells
in Trinity College
*Leabhar Cheanannais
i gColáiste na Tríonóide*

Painting from the
National Gallery
*Pictiúr ón nGailearaí
Náisiúnta*

Irish harp
Cruit

Whale skeleton
Cnámharlach de mhiol mór

Stained glass
Gloine dhaite

Top hat
Hata ard

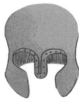

Helmet
Clogad

Peaked cap
Caipín píce

Airplane
Eitleán

Horse and carriage
Capall agus cóiste

Rosette
Róiséad

Coat of arms
Armas

Medal
Bonn

SAINT PATRICK'S DAY
LÁ FHÉILE PÁDRAIG

Wig
Bréagfholt

Bodhrán

Leprechaun
Leipreachán

Unicycle
Aonrothach

Stilts
Cosa croise

Shamrock
Seamróg

Irish dancing
Damhsa Gaelach

Ferris wheel
Roth Ferris

Balloons
Balúin

Flag
Bratach

Twirling
Ag casadh

Ship
Long

The Custom House
Teach an Chustaim

Umbrella
Scáth baistí

Life buoy
Baoi tarrthála

Bridge
Droichead

Canoeing
Canúáil

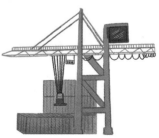

Crane and container
Crann tógála agus coimeádán

Hurley and sliotar
Camán agus sliotar

Gaelic football
Liathróid peil Ghaelach

Referee
Réiteoir

Trophy
Corn

Jersey
Geansaí

Handball
Liathróid láimhe

By the Sea...
Cois Farraige...

26

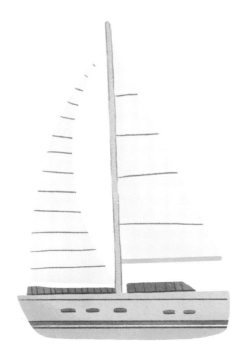

Sail boat
Bád seoil

Clouds
Scamaill

Lighthouse
Teach Solais

Seagull
Faoileán

Wind sock
Cochall gaoithe

Seal
Rón

99 cone
Cón 99

Ice-cream van
Veain uachtar reoite

Bucket and spade
Buicéad agus spád

Swimmers
Snámhaithe

Waves
Tonnta

In the Park

Ag an bpáirc

Scooter
Scútar

Swings
Luascáin

Ducks
Lachain

Flowers
Bláthanna

Swan
Eala

Ball games
Cluichí liathróide

Bench
Binse

Slide
Sleamhnán

Monkey bars
Barraí moncaí

Buggy
Bugaí

To Dylan, Maggie, Bobby and Cara, this one is for you. *Juliette*
To all who love Dublin and Ireland. *Tarsila*

JULIETTE SAUMANDE is a French writer based in Dublin. She has published over forty books in French and English, including *My Little Album of Ireland* with Tarsila Krüse. When she's not writing, she can be found translating books, reading books, recommending books, talking about books and building forts with books. She enjoys learning new things like sewing and tapdancing, she loves liquorice and gelato, but hates Crunchies with a passion. Come and say 'hi' on Facebook or Instagram @juliettesaumande

TARSILA KRÜSE is an award-winning children's book illustrator born in Brazil and based in Dublin, passionate about languages, books, drawing (and pistachio ice-cream). Tarsila is known for illustrating several books *as Gaeilge* and in English in her heartwarming, friendly and sweet style. She has also written and illustrated for the *RTÉ Christmas Guide*, Ireland's biggest-selling periodical publication (three times!) and of course, she co-authored *My Little Album of Ireland*, with Juliette Saumande.Her favourite things to draw are people and animals, especially dogs! She also loves visiting schools and libraries and facilitating book-making and illustration workshops across the Emerald Isle. You can keep up to date on Tarsila's latest work and news on her website tarsilakruse.com or social media @tarsilakruse

This paperback edition first published 2022 by The O'Brien Press Ltd,
12 Terenure Road East, Rathgar, Dublin 6, D06 HD27, Ireland
Tel: +353 1 4923333; Fax: +353 1 4922777
E-mail: books@obrien.ie Website: obrien.ie
First published in hardback in 2019 by The O'Brien Press Ltd
The O'Brien Press is a member of Publishing Ireland.

ISBN: 978-178849-348-2

6 5 4 3 2 1
25 24 23 22

Printed and bound in Poland by Bialostockie Zaklady Graficzne S.A.
The paper in this book is produced using pulp from managed forests.

Thanks very much to Marcus Mac Conghail and Sadhbh Devlin for their help with Irish vocabulary.
Ár mbuíochas le Sadhbh Devlin agus Marcus Mac Conghail as a gcúnamh leis an bhfoclóir Gaeilge.

Published in
DUBLIN
UNESCO
City of Literature

Growing up with
O'BRIEN
obrien.ie